E
CA

Cazet, Denys

Lucky me

DATE DUE		
SE 15 '89	MY 15 '93	AUG 12 97
OC 3 89	AG 12 93	APR 10 '98
	OC 25 93	AUG 31 98
JA 18 '90	APR 21 '90	
FE 17 '90	NOV 29 94	AP 08 '99	FE 27 '00
JY 23 '90	JUL 20 '95	OC 27 00	JY 11 05
OC 5 '90	JUL 22 96	JE 02 01	AG 01 18
OC 20 '90	FEB 21 '97	JY 27 01	
NO 6 '90	MAR 5 '97	JY 30 01	
MR 2 '01	MAR 26 97	AG 07 02	
SE 28 '92	JUL 07 97	AG 15 02	
	JUL 03 97	OC 17 02	

© THE BAKER & TAYLOR CO.

LUCKY ME

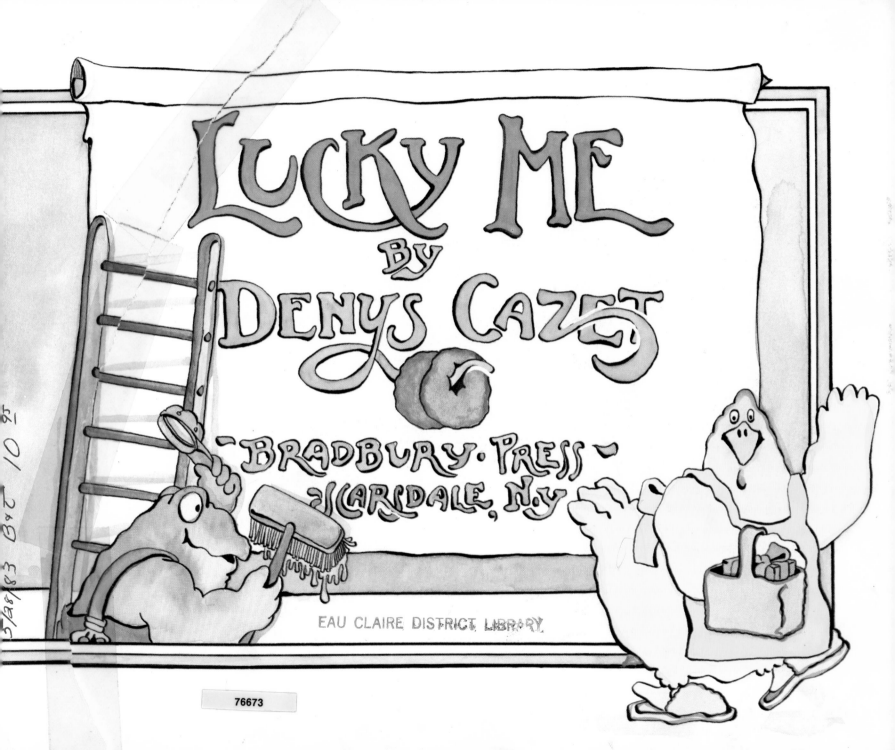

LUCKY ME

BY DENYS CAZET

- BRADBURY · PRESS -
SCARSDALE, N.Y.

The text of this book is set in 16 pt Goudy Old Style.
Library of Congress Cataloging in Publication Data
Cazet, Denys. Lucky me.
Summary: Beginning with the lucky chicken who finds a donut, each subsequent animal in this cumulative tale feels he has found a tasty morsel until an army of ants spoils the "picnic" for them all.
        [1. Animals — Fiction]   I. Title.
PZ7. C2985Lu   [E]   AACR2
ISBN 0-87888-192-1

A PUBLIC ANNOUNCEMENT
★ ★ ★
THIS BOOK IS FOR
★ ALEX ★
★
Lucky Me ♥ Denys

STAGE DO

501 THEATER

TICKETS NOW FOR THE

One spring morning a lovely chicken named Marie brought a pie to her friends, the Goslings. And the Goslings gave Marie a present for her family.

On her way home, Marie passed a bakery.

The baker gave Marie two free donuts.

"Lucky me!" said Marie.

Marie put the donuts into her bag with the present and crossed the street.

As she stepped onto the sidewalk, her heart went thump!

Marie saw a fox whose name was Flashy Jake. He was an uptown fox as slick as he was hungry. He licked his hungry lips as Marie walked by.

"Lucky me!" he said.

"Cluck!" said Marie.

Just as Flashy Jake caught up with Marie he saw a dog whose name was Truenose.

Truenose was a down and out dog with a nose for a truly tasty fox with a side order of chicken.

"Lucky me!" he said.

"Oh, oh!" said the fox.

"Cluck!" said Marie.

Just as Truenose caught up with Flashy
Jake and Marie, he saw a mountain lion
whose name was Sharpclaws.

Sharpclaws' stomach growled a hollow
growl as he stretched his long and sharp
claws.

"Lucky me!" he said.

"Yipes!" said the dog.

"Oh, oh!" said the fox.

"Cluck!" said Marie.

Just as Sharpclaws caught up with True-nose, Flashy Jake and Marie, a sourpuss of a bear came running around the corner.

His name was Munchandcrunch. A long winter's nap had made him very, very hungry.

"Yummy!" said the bear as he followed them into a park. "Just what I've been looking for . . . a four course dinner.

"Lucky me!" he said.

"Me-ow!" said the mountain lion.

"Yipes!" said the dog.

"Oh, oh!" said the fox.

"Cluck!" said Marie.

"STOP! And sit down!" shouted the bear. The others all sat down on a see-saw.

"Yum, yum, yummy," said the bear, "four tasties for brunch! Where will I start?"

"Start with the dog," said the mountain lion.

"Start with the fox," said the dog.

"Start with the chicken," said the fox.

Marie looked around. There was no one behind her except two little rabbits sitting in a sand box.

"Cluck!" said Marie.

"Hummph!" Munchandcrunch snorted. "I think I'll just sit down and study the menu."

But, as sometimes happens, the biggest did not pay attention to the smallest.

Munchandcrunch sat on the opposite end of the see-saw — but on a family of red ants!

Their names were

If you sit on us we will bite you where you sit.

And, true to their names . . .

. . . that's what they did!
  "YEEEOUCH!" screeched the bear.
He flew up into the air
and everyone else came down
with a thump on the ground.

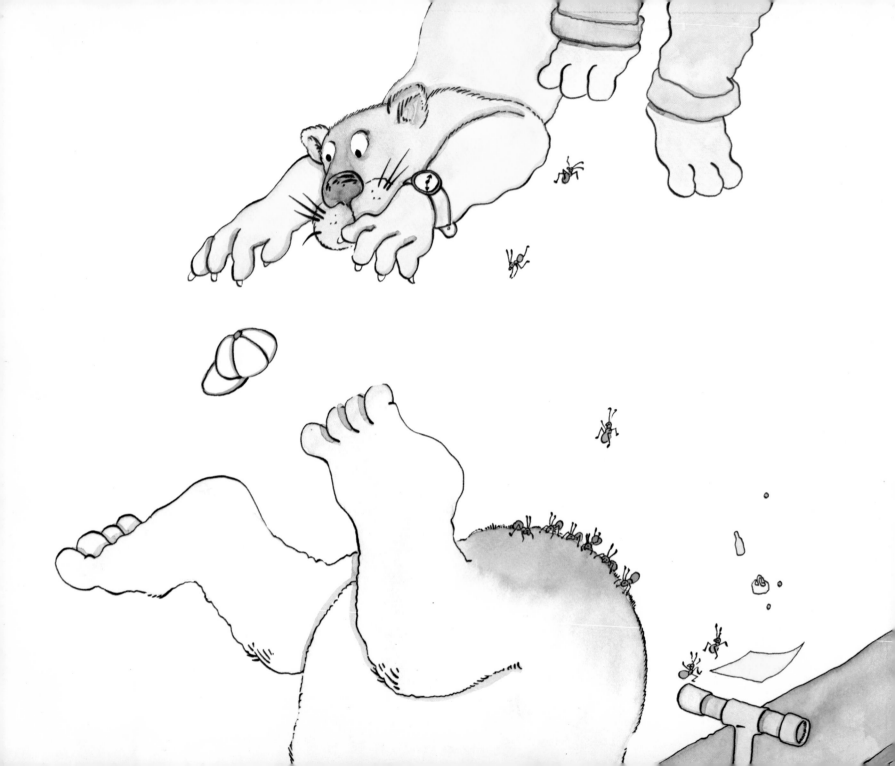

When the bear came crashing down
the others flipped up into the sky.

Marie landed in the sand box.

The dog and the mountain lion fell on top of the bear.

The fox bounced over the see-saw and ran toward the gate. "This fox is too smart to be anyone's lunch!" he shouted. "Run legs, run!"

"Bye-bye, Dullpaws!" Truenose shouted. "I'm heading home on the fastest feet in town!"

"Catch you later, Phewnose!" the mountain lion growled. "This cat isn't going to be in the middle of any fat bear's sandwich!" Sharpclaws jumped over the park wall.

Munchandcrunch shouted and stomped and slapped his bottom all the way out of the park.

Soon, it was quiet. Everyone was gone.
Except the two little rabbits.
    And the ants.
    And Marie.
    Marie took one donut out of her bag
and gave it to the two little rabbits.
    "Lucky us!" said the rabbits.
    She took the other donut out
and gave it to the ants.
    "Lucky us!" said the ants.
    "Lucky me!" said Marie.

"Home at last," smiled Marie.
"Lucky, lucky me."

"Look at what the Goslings sent us," Marie said to her family.
"DONUTS! What a nice surprise!"
  "Aren't we lucky!" said Pop Rooster.
  "Cluck!" said Marie.